George Hood

**Memorials of our Father and Mother**

also a family genealogy

George Hood

**Memorials of our Father and Mother**
*also a family genealogy*

ISBN/EAN: 9783337767518

Printed in Europe, USA, Canada, Australia, Japan

Cover: Foto ©Andreas Hilbeck / pixelio.de

More available books at **www.hansebooks.com**

# MEMORIALS

## OF OUR

# FATHER AND MOTHER.

### ALSO A

## Family Genealogy.

BY

REV. GEO. HOOD.

PHILADELPHIA:
COLLINS, PRINTER, 705 JAYNE STREET.
1867.

TO MY

BROTHERS AND SISTERS

𝕿𝖍𝖎𝖘 𝕷𝖎𝖙𝖙𝖑𝖊 𝕸𝖊𝖒𝖔𝖗𝖎𝖆𝖑 𝖁𝖔𝖑𝖚𝖒𝖊

IS

FRATERNALLY INSCRIBED.

# TO THE READER.

Tʜᴇsᴇ memorials are designed only for the eye of filial love; and should any other fall upon them, we beg such to respect this humble offering to our parents' memory, even as they did the tear we shed over their graves.

Pʀɪɴᴄᴇᴛoɴ, Nᴇw Jᴇʀsᴇʏ,
June 1, 1867.

# A Memorial of our Father.

JOHN HOOD, the subject of this sketch, was
born at Topsfield, Mass., February 26, 1760.
The place of his birth was within a hundred
feet of the western end of a small lake, in the
northwest part of the town. His parents were
small farmers, and his father a carpenter in
humble circumstances, but honorable and
pious. They were converts of Whitefield,
and were known by the conservatives of that
day as "New Lights." They were good people, and educated their family in the Puritan
faith and practice.

Our father's early education was limited to
the studies of the common schools; but in
after life he made such amends by reading as

1*

a laboring man could. He wrote a good hand, legible and neat, and his accounts were always kept in good order.

In 1775, at the age of fifteen, with his parents' approval, at the very outbreak of hostilities between England and the Colonies, he enlisted in the army of the Revolution. June 17, 1775, only fifteen years and three months old, he was at the battle of Bunker's Hill—not in the fight, but on picket duty upon the marsh near by, watching an English vessel, to keep her men from landing, with no defense from their repeated shot except a low, frail breastwork of rails and hay, behind which they lay all day in the scorching sun.

After the evacuation of Boston, Gen. Washington removed his army to Long Island. Here, August 27, 1776, another disastrous battle occurred. Our father was in it, and with our retreating army crossed over to New York. From thence our army, being flanked by the British, retreated to White Plains,

where, October 28, 1776, was fought that battle, in which also he was engaged. The American army being again defeated, re- treated, closely followed by the British, to Newark, N. J., Elizabeth, New Brunswick, Princeton, Trenton, and so into Pennsylvania; the vanguard of the English entering Trenton as our last boat landed on the Pennsylvania shore. In this famous and disastrous retreat, with all its disappointments, sufferings, and discouragements, our father partook.

After having left New Brunswick, Wash- ington's army was greatly diminished by losing the New Jersey and Maryland brigades. On the eighth of December they crossed the Delaware into Pennsylvania. With the year 1776 the term of service of the New England troops expired. The army was now separated from the victorious English only by the Dela- ware, and that was rapidly being bridged over by the frost. That crossed, and the Federal Capital, Philadelphia, was at the mercy of the

enemy. It was, therefore, necessary to retain
every man; and most of all, the New England
troops. A small bonus of a few dollars, to
supply some of their more pressing necessi-
ties, induced them to remain six weeks. The
whole campaign had been little else than a
series of disasters, and the sun of American
liberty seemed about to set in clouds of hope-
less defeat. To restore public confidence,
Washington must act. On the night of the
25th of December, 1776, at the head of 2,400
men, he recrossed the Delaware at McConkey's
Ferry, now Taylorsville, nine miles above
Trenton. The duty of boatsmen fell to Glo-
ver's regiment, to which our father belonged.
It was a stormy and bitter night, back and
forth, on that frozen river; but before day-
light the task which they alone could deftly
perform, was well done; they were all over
and on their way to Trenton, where they sur-
prised and took 1000 Hessians, arms and ar-
tillery; and marching back, recrossed the

Delaware into Pennsylvania at the same ferry, by the same faithful watermen, the same day, with their prisoners and their armament, having lost only four men. This was the golden hinge upon which turned the door to success in the American Revolution. And how much of the final issue of that hazardous undertaking hung upon the skill and endurance of that regiment we can never know.

Four days later, December 30th, Washington again recrossed the Delaware into Jersey, and occupied Trenton. Immediately the British, from New Brunswick and Princeton, moved to Trenton, January 2d, 5000 strong, and made an attack upon Washington's little army. At nightfall the firing ceased, and at one o'clock in the morning, January 3d, 1777, Washington, leaving his camp-fires burning, withdrew his army and marched to Princeton. Here a small force of British were stationed, and a battle occurred, in which our troops were victorious, taking a few prisoners, and

driving the enemy to Kingston, three miles east of Princeton, when, Washington, being pressed by the English who had rapidly pursued him from Trenton, twelve miles, turned short northward to Rocky Hill, and reached Pluckemin, in Somerset County, that evening, January 3d, having fought a battle and marched forty miles without regular sleep or food. After a brief rest he moved on to Morristown into winter quarters.

Our father was in this battle of Princeton, and in this second retreat back to nearly the same locality from which they had fled only two months before — two months of unexampled exertion, privation, and personal suffering. Without comfortable food; his clothing thin and in rags; without shoes to protect his feet from the frozen ground, his footsteps across the country marked with blood, he closed his campaign, was discharged unpaid, and without a penny to buy a loaf or a lodging, he, with several neighbors, set out for

home on foot, 250 miles, begging food and shelter as they went. Only two or three days from camp, he was taken sick of the small-pox, which at that time was a scourge in the army he had left. After having been carried for some miles from house to house, he was received at Coventry, Connecticut, and nursed by a kind old lady named Barnes; and when recovered the kind people clothed and sent him on his way to his friends, where he arrived early in the spring.

Here his stay was short. After only a few weeks he re-enlisted, and we find him marching with Washington's army the *third* time through New Jersey and Pennsylvania to Delaware, to resist the approach of the English against Philadelphia. September 11, 1777, he was at the battle of Brandywine; and with our army retreated through Chester and Philadelphia to Germantown, where he was again in battle October 4, 1777.

From Germantown they retreated to Valley

Forge, and went into winter quarters December 11th. This was the dark day of the Revolution. Never did an army suffer more or bear it more heroically. Often has the writer heard our father depict those days of suffering with no voice of complaint, but as one detailing personal suffering endured cheerfully, manfully for his country's sake. It was a cold winter, and the army was in utter destitution, with few and tattered tents, with little fuel, not half clad, many without shoes, shirts, or blankets; their clothes worn to rags, and no commissary to supply them. This was our father's case: his shoes were worthless, his shirt in rags, his clothes worn threadbare, his blanket and tent in holes, and his bed the ground, except as, by going miles, he could get a bundle of straw and take it to camp on his shoulders. His hard biscuit were often alive with worms, his drink water and his meat infrequent, scanty, and poor. Such was his life at Valley Forge.

In June Lord Howe left Philadelphia for New York, and, crossing New Jersey, desolated the country as he went. Washington also left Pennsylvania to attack him, which he did at Monmouth, June 28, 1778. Here again with the army, our father was in battle, and shortly after he was discharged a second time in New Jersey.

In the year 1779 he was out on a privateering cruise. After taking several inconsiderable prizes, they were themselves taken, carried to Halifax, and put on board the notorious Prison-ship for safe keeping, where they suffered all but death; many did die. It was the father of Libby, Belle Isle, and Andersonville, to the everlasting disgrace of the English government. After being imprisoned some months, he was exchanged and returned to his home.

In September, 1780, at the time of Arnold's treachery, he was with our troops at West Point. Again, one year later, we find him

2

with the army in Virginia, at the surrender of
Lord Cornwallis. Thus, about seven of the
eight years' war of the Revolution was our
father in active service; and although engaged at nine battles, the Lord was his shield,
not a hair of his head was hurt. And had a
parent's prayers no part in this?

Scarcely had he been at home three years,
when he was again in the field, in defence of
law and order, in his native State. Late in
1786, the organized resistance to the State
authority, known as Shay's Rebellion, broke
out, and his native town, Topsfield, was called
upon to raise troops. No one could be found
to lead in the enlistment, and utter failure
was imminent. At length, a veteran in service, though but twenty-six years old, en-
rolled his name, which was instantly followed
by the number required. This veteran was
our father. They immediately repaired to
Worcester, and were thence ordered to Spring-
field, under General Shepherd, to guard the

arsenal, and spent that intensely cold January, when it thawed not for thirty days, in western Massachusetts, discovering and arresting prominent rebels. The rebellion was quelled, and he returned to his home, having served his country with a faithful and noble devotion, still at the polls to defend the right, according to the teaching of Washington, Hancock, and Adams—a true and hearty Federalist.

Our father was twice married. His first wife was Anne Kimball, daughter of Jacob Kimball, of Topsfield. She was very attractive, and of a talented and well-educated family. They were married Aug. 2, 1787. She had one child, which died in infancy; and after two brief years of married life, she died also of consumption, Sept. 12, 1789, in the 24th year of her age. Feb. 17, 1791, he was again married to our mother, Ruth Gould.

By occupation our father was a carpenter—

that trade of all most honored—and an excel-
lent workman, though not often entering
upon enterprises of master-building or con-
tracting. His services were much sought in
bridge-building; and he helped to build seven
large bridges; over the Merrimac River, *four*,
at Andover, Haverhill, Rocks, and Plumb
Island; *one* over Parker's River at Byfield;
*one* over the Kennebec at Augusta; and *one*
over the Connecticut, at Windsor, Vermont.

His personal appearance was prepossessing.
His height was about five feet ten and a half
inches; his form erect, with a round, full
chest; his movements quick and muscular;
and his weight 160 or 170 pounds. He had
dark-brown hair, a clear skin, and ruddy coun-
tenance, with expressive dark blue eyes. His
temperament was a nervous-sanguine. His
feelings and passions were ardent; and he
was eminently social and friendly. With a
delicate nervous organism, he was always self-
possessed. A single incident will illustrate.

When, in his youth, the church was built in his native town, the tall spire was to be crowned with a weathercock. To see this put in place, the whole neighborhood had assembled. A sailor had been engaged for the work, but making the attempt his nerves failed, and no other one dared to try. Seeing none to do it, our father volunteered, ascended, put the vane in its place, waved his hat to the breathless multitude below, and descended to receive their congratulations.

As a man he was generous to a fault. He would gladly disoblige himself to oblige a friend, and enemies he had none. The warm heart, the kind word, the gentlemanly bearing, reached old and young. Little children climbed upon his knee; youth drew near his side; and age forgot its trials and fears in the sunshine of his words. How many of his younger neighbors have sincerely exclaimed: " I loved him as a father ;" and when we closed his eyes, ours wept not alone.

2*

His mind, though not remarkable for strength, was quick and observing. His combinations of thought were exceedingly rapid. Hence his rare wit, specimens of which float freely in the community in which he lived. His repartees were immediate, keen, and always tempered with kindness. Though his tongue was smooth and sharp as a sting, it had none of its poison.

From intercourse with the world, his address was above his station. It was modest, without diffidence; and easy and free, without pretension or rudeness. From much reading and a retentive memory, he was well informed, his language good and remarkably correct. His conversation was pleasing, aptly enriched with anecdotes, and often emitting the brightest scintillations of wit in happy and apposite repartee. Indeed, his whole manner and associations were above his circumstances in life.

In his family he was uniformly free and

pleasant, wearing a benevolent smile, but rarely or never laughing aloud. He seldom commanded; but his requests were fully understood and obeyed. He knew how to govern. He never allowed his children to associate with the low and debased; but encouraged them in every endeavor to attain position and influence, and rejoiced in their success.

For several years he was a careful and devoted student of the Bible. Reared in a pious family of the Puritan stamp of doctrine and practice, he was early and carefully trained to read and respect the Bible. This feeling he always retained, and doubtless its influence kept him from the vices of the camp and the world. Though not a professor of religion, he studied the Bible, in his latter years, day by day, till he obtained a good knowledge of it and of its doctrines, making quotations with remarkable freedom and accuracy. So familiar was he with it, that he

could generally tell the context of a passage, and at once turn to it. We believe he loved the truth, and was sanctified by it; for he not only read God's word, but loved and regularly attended upon public and private prayer. For years it was his daily habit to retire to a secluded spot, and there commune in secret with his God.

His last years were spent at home with his family, in the same cottage in which he was born, in which his father lived and died; which he bequeathed to his son, and which still remains in the name. There he cultivated the same land or worked at the same craft, and led the same lowly life; there he lived, and there, of violent disease, in the seventy-sixth year of his age, July 19, 1836, he died, testifying in his last words: "I know in whom I have believed."

# A Memorial of our Mother.

Ruth Gould was descended from an ancient and honorable family in our native town. Her father, Daniel Gould, was a son of John Gould, the son of the largest landholder in the town. Daniel Gould was a plain farmer, but influential and pious. In the town he held many important offices; and in the church the office of deacon for many years. He resided in the western part of the town, on the site of the original settler; that part of his grandfather's extended possessions having fallen to his father, and thus to himself. The place is owned by Capt. Israel Elliot, after being held by the Gould family near two hundred years. Here in the bosom of a family in good worldly circumstances, but *rich* in the

inheritance of Puritan faith and practice,
Ruth Gould our mother was born; and here,
except one year with an older sister, she spent
her childhood and youth till her marriage.
She was the sixth of seven children. Her
parents, DANIEL GOULD and LUCY TARBOX,
were godly people, converts of the sainted
Whitefield, as were also our father's parents.

Her person was of medium height, rather
slender, with rich light brown hair, fair skin,
and sparkling blue eyes. In her youth she
was neat and dressy, and was said to be hand-
some.

Her education, as was common in those
days, only extended to reading and writing,
and something of arithmetic, in which she was
quick and accurate. She was a good reader,
teaching all her children and giving them
their first and best impressions and habits.
We well remember standing at her knee, and
reading the Book of books under her tuition.

In early life, at the age of eighteen, she

made a public profession of religion. Hers
was a marked conversion. In deep anxiety
after a troubled night, she rose early Sabbath
morning, and for advice and direction, sought
her mother, where she knew she would find
her, even at that early hour. O, that filial
confidence, and maternal faithfulness and
piety! As she silently entered the room, her
mother was reading aloud in her morning,
secret devotions, Deut. 82, 4th: "He is the
Rock; his work is perfect; for all his ways
are judgment: a God of truth and without
iniquity, just and right is he." The passage
commanded her faith, and she was filled with
peace. The same morning, as she was entering God's House, this peace was wonderfully
increased, and her faith strengthened. Being
a little late, the Rev. Mr. Breck was just
reading that hymn of universal invitation:

> " Let every mortal ear attend,
>    And every heart rejoice,
>    The trumpet of the gospel sounds
>    With an inviting voice."

She received it as God's invitation to her, and thenceforth she was the Lord's by a living faith and constant love.

Soon after this she spent a year with her sister Lucy in Marblehead. During this time, while waiting upon her sick sister, she suddenly felt a sensation like a blow on her head. She fell, and was wholly insensible for three days, during which time, and for weeks after, her life hung by the frailest thread, being sometimes thought extinct. This providence was the means of bringing her very near to God; so much so, that her pastor, long after his removal from that field, remembered her as one of the good lambs of the flock.

In 1791, Feb. 17th, at the age of twenty-eight, she was married to our father; and soon after removed to the house of his parents, and began the sacred duties of daughter, wife, and mother. As a wife, she was a pattern of faithfulness, fidelity, frugality, and domestic virtue. She possessed a rare tact of making

the most of her little. Straitened for room,
she was ever neat, and her household appoint-
ments in careful order. With only their daily
earnings and a small farm, her appearance in
the world was worthy a better position, and
"her husband was known in the gates, when
he sat among the elders of the land." "She
sought wool and flax, and worked willingly
with her hands." "She did him good, and
not evil, all the days of her life." How much
of the well-being and respectibility of her
numerous family depended upon her energy,
discretion, good sense, and piety, we can
never know.

As a daughter to her husband's parents,
then aged and infirm, she was kind, dutiful,
and affectionate, assiduously watching their
last days and hours with a child's love.
From the first, she had their perfect confidence and truest affection. To settle in the
village had been her desire and expectation.
They had even purchased a residence there;

but the old folks found in her and in him, a
spirit so kind and congenial, that they plead,
and not in vain, for their home to be with
them; and as dutiful, unselfish, and loving
children, they gave up their own preferences,
their selected home, and fixed their abode in
our native cottage. Here she determinedly
remained, though frequent pecuniary induce-
ments urged them to leave.

As a mother, she was full of unwearied
assiduity. She knew no desire but the well-
being of her family. She had no selfish ends
or designs; no idle habits or inclinations;
she lived for her children—eminently kind
and sympathizing, and tenderly anxious for
their comfort and well-being. What un-
ceasing, uncomplaining labor, early and late!
What constant watchfulness and care!—yea,
what concern lest some want should be unsupplied, some pain unrelieved, some sorrow
unassuaged! How she watched and checked
a growing wrong, and nourished the opening

virtue! How she taught us the way of life,
pointing us heavenward and leading the
way! How sincerely she loved, how fer-
vently she prayed! Blessed be her name;
those prayers are a richer legacy to us and
our children than the mines of Peru!

Of her mental power and social habits we
may say, her mind was not more than of
medium power; nor was it greatly stored
with knowledge, other than the knowledge
of divine truth. In this she was rich. But
the ever-present desire to do right, gave her
clear perceptions of duty; and knowing that,
nothing could allure her from it.

She was energetic in action; nothing else
could have carried her through the labors
and cares of a large family of young children
and infirm age. Energy of a high character
was necessary to provide food, and raiment,
always clean and whole, if not costly. Her
executive power was far above mediocrity.
The father was away on business most of the

time for many years; and to manage all de-
partments of a large family, to provide for all
their thronging wants, to govern and to train
them to· habits of industry, to see to their
minds and morals, is no small task; and if
well done, so as to send out into the world a
well-regulated family, in spite of many adverse circumstances and influences, it is proof
of no small executive and moral power.

She was courageous, physically, but more,
morally. She never knew fear. Left with a
little family of helpless children, remote from
neighbors, fear never intruded upon her soli-
tude. Before the face of man, however suspi-
cious, she never quailed. Resolute to daring,
she commanded with such coolness and assu-
rance, that she was obeyed as though palpable
physical power were hers to enforce obedience.

But moral courage predominated. She was
always calm. No circumstances could take
from her that coolness of moral fortitude.

With a compressed lip, she met trials, difficulties, dangers, and toils, with a heroism that
in other circumstances would have been sublime.

As a Christian, she was not one to speak
freely of her feelings and experiences.
Neither was she over-reserved. Her exer-
cises of faith, hope, and love were quiet and
serene. She lived a life of faith, but exhibited
it more in her acts than by her words. She
was ever a grateful and loving Christian; and
those sentiments begat kind and loving acts.
Who of her acquaintance does not remember
her pressing hospitality, her ardent greetings,
and cheerful demeanor? Her heart was an
overflowing fountain of love, sending forth
sweet waters to refresh even the wayworn
traveller who called at her door; and fulfil-
ling most kindly and naturally the apostolic
injunction, "Be not forgetful to entertain
strangers, for thereby some have entertained
angels unawares."

3*

Perhaps in nothing was her piety more strongly or beautifully exemplified than in her care, her tender solicitude for the comfort and happiness of our grandparents. In old age, in the childhood of old age, in the decay of mind, that time often so trying to filial duty, she never wearied nor faltered. No want was unsupplied, no dropping tear unwiped. They loved her above all others, and she closed their eyes in filial, religious faithfulness and love.

But the spirit of her piety extended beyond the narrow circle of her own habitation. Deeply imbued with the spirit of the Gospel, she prayed, "Thy kingdom come," and was one of the first four Christian women in our native church to make a contribution for Foreign Missions. These four were Mrs. Dr. Cleaveland, Mrs. Jonas Merriam, Miss Abigail Perkins, and our revered mother. In making this contribution, she gave all she had, exclaiming, "It is the Lord's." Subsequently, when remembered by our Government as a

widow of a soldier of the Revolution, with a
small annuity, receiving the first payment, she
piously devoted *five dollars,* more than *one-fifth
part,* for the circulation of the Bible. Such was
her spirit of piety. The work of missions lay
near her heart; and she looked forward with
a longing faith, to the fulfilment of the rich
and glowing promises of God's word, particu-
larly loving to dwell upon the sixtieth chapter
of Isaiah.

During the last eleven years of her life, she
was confined to the house and room by means
of a fall, which, breaking the neck of the thigh
bone, lamed her for life. In all that time, she
was never once in the house of God, though,
like David, her "soul fainted for the courts of
the Lord." Her constant sitting, also, greatly
impaired her health. But though enduring
such protracted affliction, these were her happi-
est years. Used to an active life, she yielded
at once to the Divine will in a beautifully
cheerful submission. She "was afflicted, yet

she opened not her mouth." Her Bible was
her constant companion. In the eleven years
of her confinement she read it through in
course thirteen times, and the New Testa-
ment and Psalms, many more. She loved its
truths, and her soul was richly imbued with its
spirit.

But it was her last days that fully revealed
the strength of her Christian character. Then
with her Bible and her Saviour, how cheerful,
yea, how happy; under heavy affliction how
calm her faith, how steady; how tranquilly
she awaited her end; how triumphantly she
made her exit! Like Elijah, she desired to
go over Jordan alone. Her Christian heroism
set her house in order, bade farewell to her
children, dismissed them to their homes, and
then calmly awaited the summons to sleep in
Jesus. This was sublime!

Hers was a pure life and a glorious death.
Had she been surrounded by circumstances of
wealth, that the outgoings of her piety might

be seen and felt beyond the humble limits of her own cottage, hers had been accounted fame for the world to praise. But hers was a narrow sphere of action and humble. In her poverty she was not known among the great; but she was, and is, among the good. She left to her children no titles or estates; but she did leave a richer legacy than ever mere titled ancestry bequeathed, the undying fragrance of a pious life, the priceless boon of believing and prevailing prayer, to bless our children's children. Her name is fragrant in our memory. May we emulate her virtues and reap her reward!

## Our Parents.

In the preceding pages we have endeavored to give a brief view of our revered parents separately. But these memorials would still be incomplete, without a glimpse of their united lives.

John Hood and Ruth Gould were married Feb. 17, 1791; he, at the age of *thirty*, and she, at *twenty-eight*. They had eleven children. Two died in infancy, and nine lived to adult age. One was translated to her heavenly home, at the age of *twenty-six*, passing triumphantly away; and another died rich in the expectation of a mansion above, at the age of *fifty-five*.

Our parents enjoyed a long and happy matrimonial life—more than forty-five years

—with few disagreements, and no alienation.
Neither was disposed to contend, and each
was eminently unselfish. Hence each readily
yielded his own preference, and few difficulties arose. Indeed, in their daily intercourse, there was a real politeness, which,
among those in the common walks of life,
is rarely seen. **2021473**

Brought up under nearly the same family
influences, and consequently, with nearly the
same ideas of family government, their household was well ordered. They were one in
sentiment, desire, and action ; and alike intent
upon their children's obedience, politeness,
reverence for their parents, for old age, the
Sabbath, God's house, and God's word. They
tolerated no family quarrels, no domineering
disposition. Thus educated, their family
have been eminently fraternal. Few families can speak of so many in number, so long
in life, and so few interruptions of brotherly
love.

They were one in effort for their family. What he provided, she made the best use of. While he was away sometimes months, working at his trade, she was at home discreetly directing the affairs of the family and the farm. They each toiled laboriously, early and late; they were equally economical, and laid their plans with but one object, the well-being of their children.

In the education of their children they were one. With no early advantage, but the district school, they were kept constantly at that, with lessons at home, that made the school doubly effective. In the domestic education, there was no opposing precept or practice. Both parents taught diligence and economy, in time and in property. They were one to inspire their children with right views and sentiments. Whatever we are, by right teaching, and by counteracting surrounding adverse influences, they have made us. By their labors, their guidance, and by

their prayers, we have risen, while others, with far better worldly prospects, have tended downward. May we and our children prove as worthy· and useful, acting our parts as nobly as our parents; and may we bequeath as rich a legacy of faith and prayer, as we have inherited from them!

4

# A GENEALOGY

OF

# RICHARD HOOD,

WHO CAME FROM LYNN IN ENGLAND; AND SETTLED AT
LYNN IN MASSACHUSETTS, ABOUT 1650.

BY REV. GEO. HOOD.

# PREFACE.

The following Genealogy does not embrace all the families descended from Richard Hood, but only that succession in which the compiler of this work is found. Had time and means permitted, he would have gladly gathered into this work all the families descending from our common ancestor. But he has done what will enable other branches easily to arrange their lineage.

Hoping the same may be done for each family of our name, and that we may see all these lines brought together in one book; and trusting that our families may receive as much pleasure in perusing as the compiler has had in preparing this work, he cheerfully commits it to your sympathies and your keeping, that it may bear our Family Record to our children's children.

Princeton, New Jersey,
June 1, 1867.

4*

# FAMILY GENEALOGY.

PREVIOUS to the year 1650, RICHARD HOOD came from Lynn Regis, Norfolk County, England, and settled on what is now called Nahant, at Lynn, Massachusetts. He owned that peninsula. A house, with a large elm tree before it, now stands on the original site. Persecution drove him to this country, and tradition says, like many others, he was compelled to forfeit most of a large property. The settlement of his estate shows him to have been in good circumstances, leaving to each of his *thirteen* children a respectable portion. One brother came with him; but whether more than one is uncertain. It is possible there were two—John, who settled in Kittery, in Maine, before 1652, and perhaps one in

Boston. But this is not probable, inasmuch as
the names of Richard and John only are found
on the old records.

1. Richard Hood was born at Lynn Regis,
Norfolk County, England, about the year
1630 or 1632, and died at Lynn, Massachusetts,
September 12, 1695, aged sixty-three or sixty-
five years. His wife's name was Mary; but *Hawgall*
her maiden name, or when or where she was *Ann Guthray*
born or married, is unknown to the writer.
He died first, and his son John settled the
estate. Their children were:—

| | | | |
|---|---|---|---|
| 2. Richard | . . . | born about ~~1660.~~ *Sept. 14, 1655* | |
| 3. John . | . . . | " ~~1668.~~ *March 7, 1664.* | |
| 4. Samuel | . . . | " " ~~1670.~~ *May 12, 1667—* | |
| 5. Nathaniel | . . . | " " ~~1672.~~ *June 9, 1669* | |
| 6. Joseph | . . . | " July 8, 1674. | |
| 7. Benjamin | . . . | " Jan. 3, 1677. | |
| 8. Mary . | . . . | when born unknown. | |
| 9. Sarah . | . . . | " " *June 2, 1657—* | |
| 10. Eliza . | . . . | " " | |
| 11. Ruth . | . . . | " " | |
| 12. Rebecca | . . . | " " *Dec. 7, 1662—* | |
| 13. Hannah | . . . | " " *Aug. 21, 1665—* | |
| 14. ~~Emma~~ *Anna* . | . . . | " " *Dec. 13, 1672* | |

Where Joseph or Benjamin resided is to the author unknown. It is probable, however, that at least one of them settled in Boston, a ship-carpenter, and gave origin to the families of our name still living there; and that thus these families sprang directly from Richard Hood (1).

Richard, John, and Samuel united with the Society of Friends or Quakers, before the year 1690; and from that year to 1720 they made a yearly petition to have their minister tax refunded. In 1696, John Hood was imprisoned one month in Salem jail for refusing to pay a tax to support the Rev. Mr. Shepherd. A son or grandson of his was a well-known Quaker minister in Lynn for many years.

Concerning the daughters, there is neither history nor tradition. Their names, taken from an inventory of the settlement of their father's estate, doubtless stand in the order of their ages, but the date of their birth is unknown.

## Second Generation.

RICHARD HOOD (2), eldest son of Richard Hood (1), the first settler in Lynn, was married about 1689. He had three sons; but whether any daughters is uncertain. His descendants still live on the Nahant. His children were:—

15. SAMUEL, born Oct.  18, 1690.
16. RICHARD,  "  March 30, 1692.
17. ZEBULON,  "  Feb.  28, 1694, died July 12, 1695.

———

JOHN HOOD (3), second son of Richard Hood (1), was born about 1668. He lived in Lynn. His wife's name was Sarah. Their children were:—

18. BARBARY  .  .  . born July 10, 1694.
19. HULDAH  .  .  .  "  Nov. 28, 1697.
20. BENJAMIN  .  .  .  "  June  1, 1700.
21. CONTENT  .  .  .  "  Aug. 25, 1703.
22. BREED  .  .  .  "  Aug. 21, 1706.
23. LYDIA  .  .  .  "  April 17, 1714.

NATHANIEL HOOD (5), the fourth son of Richard Hood (1), was born about 1672, and was married October 16, 1706, with Joanna Dunnell, or Dwinell, of Topsfield. She died March 1, 1732; and he died October 30, 1748, aged about 76 years. For a time he lived in Lynn, and his elder children were born there; but he removed from Lynn to Topsfield in 1712, and settled in the extreme northwest part of the town, adjoining Ipswich and Boxford. Tradition says, he also, with his brothers, became a Quaker. This is not certain. His children were not baptized according to custom; but none of them were Quakers. It is probable that the influences which proselyted his brothers, together with their legal difficulties with the parish on account of the minister tax, led him to neglect the baptism of his children, and perhaps other ordinances of the parish church. But there is no evidence that he ever joined the Quakers. His children were:—

24. NATHAN,    born 1702.   Died      1788.
25. NATHANIEL,   "   1704.    " June 8, 1755.
26. RICHARD,     "
27. JOSEPH,      "
28. SUSANNAH    "
29. AMOS,·      "
30. JOHN, born Jan. 10, 1724.   Died Oct., 1805.

Richard and Joseph were married, but their families have become extinct. Susannah married a Mr. Cummings, resided at Stoughton, Mass., and lived to a great age. Amos was a bachelor, and resided at Biddeford, Maine.

## Third Generation.

NATHAN HOOD (24), eldest son of Nathaniel Hood (5) and Joanna Dwinell, married Elizabeth Palmer. They resided at Topsfield, Mass. Their children were:—

31. WILLIAM,    .   .    born Jan. 17, 1732.
32. MARY,   .    .   .     "   Jan. 1, 1736.
33. MEHITABLE,   .    .     "
34. NATHAN    .   .     "   Jan. 5, 1740.
35. DANIEL,     .   .     "   Nov. 6, 1741.
36. HANNAH,    .   .     "
37. JOSEPH,     .   .     "   Feb. 10, 1746.
38. ELIZABETH   .   .     "   April 14, 1750.

NATHANIEL HOOD (25), second son of Nathaniel Hood (5) and Joanna Dwinell, married
Abigail Potter, November 13, 1735. They
had seven children; three died in infancy, and
four daughters lived and were married. Here
the name of this family became extinct. The
daughters names were:—

*Samuel*      *1737*
40. ESTHER,    .    .    born May 20, 1739.
41. ABIGAIL    .    .    "    May 16, 1741.
42. SARAH,    .    .    "    *1743-*
43. SUSANNAH,    .    .    "    Oct. 27, 1745.

*2) Sarah married Alexander Tapley, Dec. 9, 1762—*
*1) Susanna " Smart Kenney, June 9, 1763—*

JOHN HOOD (30), of Topsfield, youngest son
of Nathaniel Hood (5), and Joanna Dwinell,
was twice married. His first wife was Elizabeth Redington. They had four children—
three died in infancy, and one survived.

44. RICHARD, born March 1, 1751. Died Nov. 19, 1836.

Elizabeth Redington Hood died Oct. 23,
1755.

John Hood (30), married a second wife,
Mary Kimball, March 1, 1757. She died the.
*Oct. 10, 1756 — 1) Jan. 1757 Topsfield V R*
5

*She was born Aug. 25, 1727—*

death of the righteous, Dec. 6, 1807, aged 82 years. Their children were:—

45. Eunice, born Oct. 1, 1757. Died Oct. 11, 1790.
46. John, " Feb. 26, 1760. " July 19, 1836.
47. Samuel, " Mar. 1, 1762. " Dec. 10, 1843.
48. Hulldah," May 27, 1765. " Feb. 18, 1776.
49. Esther, " Sept. 4, 1768. " Sept. 25, 1775.

## Fourth Generation.

Richard Hood (44), son of John Hood (30), and Elizabeth Redington, married Lydia Tarbox, Feb. 1775. She was born Sept. 16, 1753, and died March 10, 1824. He died Nov. 19, 1835. They resided at Wenham, Massachusetts. Their children were:—

50. Josiah Moulton, born July 22, 1776. Died Aug. 1865.
51. Betsy, " Mar. 6, 1778. " Jan. 1840.
52. John, " Feb. 4, 1780. " Feb. 8, 1781.
53. Mary, " July 27, 1783. " Dec. 8, 1807.
54. Samuel, " Nov. 8, 1785. " June 1843.

Eunice Hood (45), eldest daughter of John Hood (30), and Mary Kimball, married Henry

Perley, of Boxford, where they resided. She died Oct. 11, 1790, aged thirty-three years. Their children were:—

55. Eunice, born April 14, 1782. Died July 18, 1862.
56. Henry, " Oct. 14, 1784. " Nov. 14, 1841.
    Susannah, " Feb. 17, 1789. " Nov. 23, 1791.
57. Samuel, " Oct. 9, 1790. "

————

John Hood (46), eldest son of John Hood (30), and Mary Kimball, was twice married. His first wife, Anne Kimball, was born June 2, 1765. They were married Aug. 2, 1787, and had one child, which died in infancy. She died Sept. 12, 1789.

His second wife, Ruth Gould, was born Dec. 3, 1762. They were married *She died March 8, 1840* Feb. 17, 1791. They resided at Topsfield, Massachusetts. Their children were:—

58. Jacob, born Dec. 25, 1791. Died *Jan. 17, 1886 —*
59. John, " Oct. 8, 1793. " *March 12, 1870*
60. Anne, " July 29, 1795. " *Oct. 18, 1874 —*
61. Ruth, " July 29, 1795. " Dec. 23, 1821.
62. David, " Sept. 3, 1797. " Mar. 22, 1852.

63. RICHARD, born Sept. 4, 1799.   Died Nov. 8, 1799.
64. MARY,      "   Sept. 29, 1800.   "  *Sept. 27, 1875 =*
65. RICHARD,   "   Dec. 9, 1802.    "  *April 20, 1881 —*
66. GEORGE,    "   Aug. 11, 1805.   "   Oct. 5, 1805.
67. GEORGE,    "   Feb. 10, 1807.   "  *Sept. 24, 1882 —*
68. LUCY,      "   June 25, 1809.   "

SAMUEL HOOD (47), youngest son of John Hood (30), and Mary Kimball, married Lydia Gould, July 22, 1783. She was born Dec. 31, 1760, and died Dec. 2, 1834. They resided at Topsfield, Mass. Their children were:—

69. SAMUEL,      born Nov. 24, 1784.   Died Aug. 29, 1865.
70. LYDIA,        "   Sept. 13, 1786.   "   Nov. 1, 1859.
71. NELLY,        "   Apr. 13, 1789.    "
72. ELISHA,       "   Dec. 13, 1796.    "   Jan. 15, 1830.
73. EDWARD,       "   May 1, 1799.      "   Aug. 21, 1852.
74. JOHN GOULD,   "   June 4, 1807.     "   June 6, 1858.

## Fifth Generation.

JACOB HOOD (58), eldest son of John Hood (46), and Ruth Gould, was married to Sophia Needham, daughter of Daniel Needham and Edia Flint, June 1, 1820. She was born at

*Rev. Jacob Hood died Jan. 17, 1886 —*
*Sophia Needham Hood died Dec. 14, 188*

Lynnfield, Mass., Jan. 1, 1797. For many years he was a teacher at Salem, Mass., where his children were born; then became acting pastor of an Orthodox Congregational Church at Nottingham, N. H., and now resides at Lynnfield Centre, and is acting pastor of a church in that town. Their children are:—

75. JACOB AUGUSTINE, born May 5, 1822. D. *July 9, 1890*
76. ELIZABETH SOPHIA, " Mar. 16, 1824. " *July 12, 1879*
77. MARY JANE, " Nov. 23, 1827. "
78. SARAH NEEDHAM, " Aug. 21, 1829. "Aug. 31, 1830.
79. SARAH F. NEEDHAM," Aug. 22, 1831. "
80. DANIEL NEEDHAM, " Sept. 25, 1833. "
81. GEORGE HENRY, " May 30, 1835. "

JOHN HOOD (59), second son of John Hood (46), and Ruth Gould, was married to Elizabeth B. Phillips, Dec. 20, 1854. She was born Dec. 2, 1819, and died in the Lord Dec. 17, 1859. They had no children.

ANNE HOOD (60), eldest daughter of John Hood (46), and Ruth Gould, married Zaccheus

REMARKABLE OCCASION. On Thursday, June 1, occurred the 62d anniversary of the marriage of Rev. Jacob Hood and wife, now of Lynnfield, formerly of Salem. The event was commemorated by a pleasant family

GOLDEN WEDDING. On Thursday, June 1, occurred the 50th anniversary of the marriage of Rev. Jacob Hood and wife, now of Lynnfield, formerly of Salem. The event was commemorated by a pleasant family gathering at the homestead, in which the governments referred to and by numerous congratulatory visits from neighbors and friends, accompanied by a needful banquet over which the patriarch invoked a devout blessing, a profusion of tender flowers gladdened the eye and filled the room with perfume, and a general joyousness pervaded the company, moistened by any differences of formality in the proceedings.

It is seldom that a wedded pair strives to celebrate an anniversary period of married life, and still more rare that an occurrence so remarkably well preserved and so vigorous. Both were born on successive Christmas days, Mr. Hood, in Topsfield, on Christmas day, December 25, 1791, and his wife, Lucinda, in New York day, January 1, 1799, he being now in his 84th year and she in her 76th. Their descendants number six children, five of whom are living; and 23 grandchildren, 23 of whom are living; and 3 great-grandchildren—a remarkable progeny. Their grandchildren are grandchildren of the oldest and honored Lieut. Col. Benj. F. Martin, who fell at Newbern, N. C., in 1862.

Mr. Hood was for many years a faithful servant of Christ. In course to Salem in 1829, and was Principal of the East and South Schools for a considerable period, and the practical education derived from his tuition has been amply demonstrated in the after life of many of his pupils, comprising not unfavorably with that of those who have been subjected to the enlarged scope of the public schools of the present day.

In his long and useful life the venerable teacher has been constantly engaged, respected for his own family, and for the community. After leaving the public schools he was a teacher of evangelistic labors, and for some time an agent of the American Bible Society. For a long period he was the leader of the Salem Church Choir in this city, which large choirs and sacred music were the foundation in churches, and his success in that department, aided by a musically gifted family, was marked and memorable.

In 1865 he was ordained as a minister, and had charge of a Lynnfield Congregational Church for several years. In 1872, when his Golden Wedding was celebrated, he was enabled to join the three miles to church every Sunday, conduct two services, and superintend the Sabbath School. He has reached by Lynnfield since 1865.

None who saw the venerable couple on this occasion could fail to recognize, with George Herbert, that "age is not all decay; it is the ripening, the swelling, of the fresh life within, that withers and bursts the husks," or to foresee that

"an old age serene and bright,
Will lead them to the grave."

Before separating, the company gathered about the doorstep, as the shadows broke away, and the sun illumined the western sky, sang the dear old hymn, with which was composed by Mr. Hood, and, joining the hands and raising their sacred trust, more than three score years, a dozen voices farewell, departed to their several homes. Long may the venerable couple survive, surrounded and blessed in their retirement and age, while,

"that which should accompany old age,
As honor, love, obedience, troops of friends,"

Gould, of Topsfield, Nov. 2, 1812. He was born Jan. 19, 1790. *Died July 5, 1874 —* Their children are:—

*She died Oct. 18, 1874 —*

| | | |
|---|---|---|
| 82. ANNE, | born June 24, 1813. | D. June 8, 1846. |
| 83. ZACCHEUS, | " April 3, 1815. | " |
| 84. ADELINE, | " Feb. 28, 1817. | " *July 5, 1892 —* |
| 85. REBECCA, | " Apr. 28, 1819. | " Aug. 12, 1843. |
| 86. EMILY, | " Apr. 5, 1821. | " *Oct. 1876 —* |
| 87. JOHN, | " Jan. 30, 1824. | " |
| 88. ELIZABETH, | " June 28, 1826. | " Nov. 13, 1827. |
| 89. HUMPHREY, | " Oct. 13, 1829. | " Nov. 12, 1856. |
| 90. ELIZABETH, | " July 8, 1832. | " |
| 91. WM. H. HARRISON, | " June 25, 1836. | " |

---

DAVID HOOD (62), third son of John Hood (46), and Ruth Gould, whose name was changed by an act of the legislature of Massachusetts, to Westley De La Fletcher, was married to Phebe Foster, daughter of Thomas Foster, of Linebrook parish, in Ipswich, Mass., June 5, 1820. She was born at Ipswich, Jan. 27, 1797. *Died Sept. 29, 1875 —* Their children are:—

| | | |
|---|---|---|
| 92. ELIZA CHARLOTTE, | born Dec. 15, 1820. | D. Feb. 3, 1866. |
| 93. SALMON DUTTON, | " Feb. 17, 1830. | " |

RICHARD HOOD (65), fifth son of John Hood (46), and Ruth Gould, was married to Asenath Smith, Sept. 22, 1825. She was born Sept. 21, 1798, and died Oct. 4, 1859, at Danvers, Mass., where he resides.

He was married to Harriet Parker, of Groton, Mass., Jan. 27, 1861. She was born Jan. 28, 1834.

His children by Asenath Smith, are:—

94. RICH. BRAINARD, born Jan. 31, 1826. D. *Aug. 16, 1889*
95. RUTH, " June 30, 1827. " *July 5, 1872.*
96. FRANCES MELVENA " Jan. 4, 1829. "
97. WILLIAM ORVIN, " May 4, 1830. "
98. ADONIRAM JUDSON, " Apr. 7, 1832. "
99. ELSA ASENATH, " Jan. 10, 1834. " Jan. 14, 1835.
100. ALONZO LE ROY, " Aug. 7, 1836. " Jan. 18, 1837.
101. MARY ASENATH, " Apr. 25, 1838. "
102. ALONZO LE ROY, " Apr. 30, 1840. " Sept. 4, 1840.

His children by Harriet Parker are:—

103. WALLACE PARKER, born Dec. 3, 1863. D.

———

GEORGE HOOD (67), seventh son of John Hood (46), and Ruth Gould, was married at Newark, Del., to Martha Ann Bell, Dec. 26,

1844. She was the daughter of the Rev. Samuel Bell and Mary Snodgrass, and was born in Newcastle County, Delaware, April 27, 1819. · Their children are :—

104. GEORGE ALFRED, born at Philadelphia, Pa., July 13, 1846. D.
105. EDWARD CLEEVES, " Lawrenceville, Pa., Apr. 21, 1848. D.
106. MARY GOULD, " Bath, N. Y., Mar. 10, 1850. D.
107. EMMÁ, " Southport, N. Y., Mar. 8, 1852. D.
108. JOHN HAMILTON, " Newark, Del., Oct. 24, 1857. Died May 24, 1858.
109. CHARLES HOWARD, " Chester, Pa., July 14, 1860. D.

## Sixth Generation.

JACOB AUGUSTINE HOOD (75), eldest son of Jacob Hood (58), was born in Marblehead, May 5, 1822. He was graduated at Dartmouth College in 1844, and at Union Theological Seminary, in New York City, in 1849; ordained and installed pastor of the Orthodox Congregational Church in Middletown, Mass.,

Jan. 2, 1850; was, at his own request, dismissed, June, 1854; was installed pastor of the Congregational Church in Pittsfield, N. II., Dec. 12, 1854; was again dismissed at his own request in June, 1862; and became acting pastor of the two Congregational Churches in Loudon, N. II., July 1, 1862. *He died July 9, 1890 Schuyler, Nebraska*

December 27, 1849, he married Kate Delia, daughter of Jacob M. and Eleanor (Randall) Hawkins. She was born in Scottstown, Orange County, N. Y., Nov. 18, 1830; and died at Pittsfield, N. II., March 29, 1857.

Sept. 24, 1857, he married Emily Parker, daughter of Oliver P. and Charlotte Mayo (Fay) Greene. She was born in Pittsfield, N. II., May 9, 1838.

By Kate Delia his children were:—

110. AUGUSTINE HAWKINS, born in Middletown, Mass., Sept. 30, 1850.          Died

111. ELLEN RANDALL, born at Middletown, Feb. 5, 1853.
          Died

112. KATE NEEDHAM,  "  "  Pittsfield, N. II., Dec. 11, '56.
          Died *April 19, 1876 Lynnfield, Mass.*

By Emily Parker he had *thee* ~~one~~ childr~~en~~

113. HERBERT FAY, born at Pittsfield, N. H., Aug. 16, 1858.
Died *Feb. 8, 1884 —*

*Harriet Flint, born Aug. 20, 1870, at Macon, Illia*
*Florence, b. April 9, 1877, at Schuyler, Neb. d. April 22, 18*

ELIZABETH SOPHIA HOOD (76), daughter
of Jacob Hood (58), married, July 11, 1843,
Henry Merritt, son of David and Anne (Ashby)
Merritt. He was born at Marblehead, June 4,
1819. At the call of his country, he entered
the service, was commissioned Lieut.-Colonel
of the 23d Regiment of Massachusetts Volun-
teers, Sept. 1861, and fell leading on his regiment at the battle of Newberne, N. C., March
14, 1862. Their children, born at Salem,
are:—

114. HENRY AUGUSTINE, born June 15, 1845.  D. *Oct. 12, 1891.*
115. LIZZIE SOPHIA,      "  Sept. 17, 1848.  "
116. WALTER HOWARD,      "  Aug. 26, 1852.  "

*Known as Jennie Hood —*
MARY JANE HOOD (77), second daughter of
Jacob Hood (58), married George Chapman

(114) Henry Augustine Merritt married
Lucinda F. Symonds, Salem, Aug. 1, 1876.
Two sons, born in Salem.

(115) Lillie Celia Merritt married
Charles H. Fadd. Salem Sept. 3, 1878.
She is now Elizabeth Merritt Godda.

(116) Hattie Howard Merritt married
her cousin, uncle, Lynn, Apr. 30, 1890.

(117) Jennie Boyd Weddin &c. May 25, 1870,
Frederick William Hutel, born in Bath, Me.
April 14, 1845. Son of William Boyd,
and Sarah (Hunter) Hutel.

(118) Albert David Weddin married
May 18, 1887, Alice Lavinia Campbell,
born April 9, 1866 in Chelsea. Daughter of
Charles F. & Lavinia (Hutchinson) Campbell.

Campbell. born Chelsea, Nov. 18, 1888.

(119) Harry Palfray Boldero m. Chelsea
April 26, 1883, Florence Richmond Eustis
b. June 7, 1861 in Chelsea   Daughter of
James C. F. and Annie (Pratt) Eustis.

Eustis.   Born Chelsea Feb. 8, 1884
George Chapman 3d b. Reading, Oct. 11
Genevieve, born Reading Aug. 14, 189_

(120) Frederick Needham Boldero, married
Caroline Augusta Goodridge, April 27, 1882.
Born in Boston, Aug. 20, 1860 —
Daughter of James Jasper Goodridge and
Margaret Augusta Harley —

Amy Goodridge, born Medford, Nov. 19, 1888

(121) George Chapman Boldero Jr. m.
Lawrence, Dec. 14, 1887, Mary Emma Fisher,
born in Lawrence, Nov. 30, 1866.  Daughter of
James Crumleigh & Emma (Abbott) Fisher

(124) Nettie Greenough Hood marr[?]
Frank D. Emerson, Rockford, Dec. 25, 187[?]
Ernest, born Rockford, Ill. May 29, 1882 –
Frederick, Hood, born [?] April 14, 1884,




Genevieve Hood marr[?] Sept. 6, 1892
, Greenleaf Campbell of Chelsea, Ma[?]




(128) Frederic Clark Hood marr[?]
in Providence, Nov. 4, 1891, Alyea Peck[?]

*Jonathan*

Bosson, son of Benjamin Davis and Lydia (Palfray) Bosson, May 10, 1849. He was born at Charlestown, Mass., Oct. 11, 1825. He is a commission merchant in Boston, residing in Chelsea. Their children are:—

117. JENNIE HOOD,        born Feb. 26, 1850.  D.
118. ALBERT DAVIS,         "   Nov.  8, 1853.  "
119. HARRY PALFRAY,        "   Feb. 26, 1857.  "
120. FREDERICK NEEDHAM, "   Dec. 15, 1860.  "
121. GEORGE CHAPMAN,       "   June 11, 1865.  "

——

SARAH NEEDHAM HOOD (79), daughter of Jacob Hood (58), married, Aug. 11, 1853, Edward Augustus Webster, son of Stephen and Abigail (Messer) Webster. He was born in Salem, Mass., Feb. 15, 1824. He is an agent, and resides in Chicago, Ill. Their children are:—

122. STEPHEN AUGUSTUS, born at Salem, June 12, 1856.
                                                Died
123. ELIZABETH WALKER, "   " Beloit, Wis., Jan. 9, 1858.
                                                Died

(122)- Stephen M. Webster married Aug. 15, 1892
         Estelle A. Goodwell of Galesburg, Illinois-

(123) Elizabeth W. Webster, married
         Frank M. Hughes, of Schuyler, Nebraska
         Mabelle, born April 28, 1890 -
              "    July 5, 1892 -

DANIEL NEEDHAM HOOD (80), son of Jacob
Hood (58), married, June 9, 1853, Maria Jen-
nette, daughter of John Grafton and Jennette
(Putnam) Greenough. She was born in South
*She died Feb. 21, 1860, in St. Augustine, Florida*
Boston, Jan. 29, 1835. He is a Professor of
Music in Rockford (Ill.) Female Seminary.
Their children are:—

124. NETTIE GREENOUGH, born in Brooklyn, N. Y., Jan. 25,
      1855. Died
125. CARRIE FRANCIS, born in Rockford, Ill., Oct. 4, 1858..
      Died *May 20, 1860, in St. Augustine, Florida*

*Genevieve Maria — Rockford Sept. 9, 1871 —*

*He married Mrs. Nellie (Burton) Blodgett, June 29, 1881 —*

GEORGE HENRY HOOD (81), son of Jacob
Hood (58), married, Sept. 18, 1859, Frances
Henrietta, daughter of Dennis and Sarah
(Knowles) Janvrin. She was born in Chelsea,
June 29, 1839. He is a commission merchant
in Boston, residing in Chelsea. Their chil-
dren are:—

126. HELEN FRANCES, born June  28, 1860. D.
127. GEORGE HENRY,   "   Oct.   1, 1862.  " *Dec. 27, 1865*
128. FREDERIC CLARK,  "   March 11, 1865.  "

*Arthur Needham, Feb. 15, 1868 —*
*Richard Kneeland, Aug. 5, '71 —*
*Florence Henrietta, May 11, 1876 —*

ELIZA CHARLOTTE HOOD (92), daughter of
David or Westley De La Fletcher Hood (62),
was married to William Hall, of Ipswich,
Jan. 13, 1848. Their children are:—

129. EDWARD CLARANCE, b. May 31, 1850. D.
130. ALICE GREENWOOD, " Dec. 25, 1860. " Feb. 21, 1866.

An infant son was born Oct. 26, 1855, and
died March, 1856.

———

SALMON DUTTON HOOD (93), son of David
(62) and Phebe, Hood, married Perthena Ca-
lista Pearson, March 31, 1850. She was born
at Ipswich, Jan. 28, 1833. They reside at
Topsfield, Mass. Their children are:—

131. ELENOR JENNESS, born June 24, 1853. D.
132. WILBUR FLETCHER, " Nov. 6, 1855. "
133. ELIZA CHARLOTTE, " Dec. 29, 1857. "
134. SUSAN ISABEL, " Feb. 9, 1863. "
*Ralph Button* // *Aug. 28, 1874 —*

———

RICHARD BRAINARD HOOD (94), son of Richard Hood (65) and Asenath Smith, was mar-
⁶ *He died Aug. 16, 1889 —*

ried to Louisa Jane Webber, May 28, 1848. She was born at Chaply, Me., May 14, 1826. They reside in Danvers, Mass. Their children are:—

135. FRANKLIN EDSON, born Feb. 2, 1850. D.
136. FRED BRAINARD, " July 20, 1858. "

———

RUTH HOOD (95), eldest daughter of Richard Hood (65) and Asenath his wife, was married at Danvers, with Ebenezer Bolls Buxton, April 30, 1848. He was born at Richmond, N. H., May 7, 1824. They reside at North Reading, Mass. Their children are:—

137. MARY SUSAN, born Sept. 20, 1849. D.
138. CHARLES ADAMS, " April 18, 1851. "
139. RICHARD HOOD, " May 16, 1853. "
140. ALBERT HENRY, " Sept. 21, 1854. "
141. ELSIE ASENATH, " Feb. 10, 1868. "

———

FRANCES MALVENA HOOD (96), second daughter of Richard (65) and Asenath Hood, was married with Charles Adams, May 5,

1848. IIe was born at Brookfield, Mass., Dec. 28, 1826, and died at Atlanta, Ga., Oct. 5, 1865. Their children are:—

142. ADDIE FRANCES, born at Danvers,     Sept. 5, 1849.
     Died
143. CHARLES FRANCIS, "  " Malone, N.Y., April 22, 1852.
     Died July 5, 1866.
144. SAMUEL HAMILTON, "  " Hamilton, C.W., Sept. 12, '54.
     Died
145. CARRIE BELL,     "  " Racine, Wis.,  Feb. 9, 1857.
     Died
146. GEORGE MOBB, b. at Elizabethtown, Ky., July 5, 1860.
     Died

Addie Frances Adams (142) was married with Harry Van Allen McCrea, of Chattam, C. W., Nov. 18, 1865.

———

WILLIAM ORVIN HOOD (97), second son of Richard Hood (65), was married with Martha Caldwell, Feb. 13, 1856. She was born at Beverly, Mass., Nov. 5, 1833. They reside in Danvers, Mass. Their children are:—

147. CHARLES WILLIAM, born Dec. 20, 1860.  D.
148. CLARENCE ORVIN,   "  Sept. 11, 1863.  "

ADONIRAM JUDSON HOOD (98), third son of
Richard Hood (65), was married to Catharine
Reynolds Porter, Jan. 9, 1855. She was born
at Beverly, July 17, 1833. They reside at
Danvers, Mass.

———

MARY ASENATH HOOD (101), fourth daughter of Richard Hood (65), was married with
Leonard C. Legro, Dec. 22, 1857. He was
born May 8, 1834. They reside at Lynn,
Mass. Their children are :—

149. JAMES,          born Jan. 25, 1858.  Died Oct. 5, 1858.
150. LIZZIE,           "   Aug. 30, 1859.   "
151. ANTHON PORTER, "   Oct.  2, 1862.   "